THE MAN WHO REMEMBERED THE MOON

THE MAN WHO REM- EMB- ERED THE MOON

DAVID HULL

D DUMAGRAD
TORONTO

First published in 2015
Dumagrad Books
Toronto
dumagrad.com
info@dumagrad.com

Cover by David Drummond
Salamander Hill Design

Printed and bound in Canada
Coach House Printing, Toronto

LIBRARY AND ARCHIVES CANADA
CATALOGUING IN PUBLICATION

Hull, David, author
The man who remembered the moon / by David Hull.

Issued in print and electronic formats.
ISBN 978-0-9937909-0-4 (pbk.)
ISBN 978-0-9937909-1-1 (html)

I. Title.

PS8615.U43M36 2015   C813'.6   C2015-902130-8
C2015-902131-6

There is nothing so beautiful as that which does not exist.

– PAUL VALERY

THE MAN WHO REMEMBERED THE MOON

CAN YOU IMAGINE how you would study the face of someone you loved if she was about to depart on a journey from which you knew she'd never return? Or how you would try to recall her if you learned, sometime after your last glimpse of her, that you would never see her again?

That's how I summon the moon: I squeeze my eyes shut and will it into being. And that's how I studied it, the last time I saw it: I remember how it struck me so suddenly, how I paused and drank it in with such deliberate interest (how often did you—if you remember the moon—how often did you stop in your tracks and stare at it?); and I still ask myself: did I somehow know it was going to vanish?

It rose after 11 PM, and loomed over the skyline, an enormous oblate copper dwarfing the towers downtown. I stopped; I beheld; I felt an infusion of cosmological awe; then I moved on, the moon and moment forgotten. But two or three hours later, when I stepped out on the fire escape for a cigarette, the moon was gone.

I wasn't alarmed. I simply assumed it was hidden behind a cloud that had camouflaged its own passage through darkness so well that the cloud itself was not visible. Or that I'd underestimated the moon's pace as it tacked the ecliptic, and it was now somewhere out of sight in the west…

Talk like that never fails to perk up my doctor. I sometimes catch him drifting. So it's gratifying when I snag his wandering thoughts and reel them back in. His eyes light up, his countenance brightens, the energy drained away by my monotonous litany surges back as though I've touched the key that awakens him from sleep mode.

"The—ecliptic? Is that the word you used? What's that?" he asked, hoisting himself up with his elbows. "The ecliptic. Sounds—sexual?"

"This you should know," I said. "It's the path the sun traces through the sky. The moon followed it too."

Pallister beamed, as one would for an especially delightful improvisation by a precocious, yarn-spinning child. "The moon followed the same path as the sun?"

"Within a few degrees. It traced a shallow sine wave over it."

"But…" He frowned, and his eyes slid out of focus as he strained to visualize this in his mental construct of the solar system. "But how could that be? You said it orbited the earth, and we agree the earth orbits the sun. How could…" He held up his hands and let one of them slowly circle the other, which in turn he moved on an even slower tangential arc. Then raised his palms in a shrug and looked at me as though he'd at last demonstrated, conclusively, the absurdity of my belief.

I was going to go through the basketball-baseball-golf ball thing again. But suddenly I felt weary and hopeless. It was just too complicated.

o

I SAW THE MOON for the last time on a Tuesday, but it wasn't until the next night that I realized it was really gone. I was with Helen. We'd made love in the hot bedroom and then fled to the fire escape to dry off. The June air was warm and still and the stars were blurry approximations through the city's heated atmosphere. The clock in the kitchen said midnight.

I opened a can of Guinness, waited as the oxygen gadget in the base burst and aerated the beer, tipped my head back for my first swig, and saw—nothing. Very conspicuous by its absence was the moon.

"Where's the moon?" I asked.

I looked this way and that. I squinted, peering for clouds in greasepaint. I looked at Helen. I didn't expect her to find its absence immediately noteworthy, because the moon was such a—such a commonplace. Most people never paid much attention to it, in the sense that if you polled the planet at noon, asking whether the moon was out last night, three quarters wouldn't have known. ("Let me get this straight. Everyone knew about it and it was huge. And nobody noticed if it was there or not." My doctor again, with a certain glee.) So I was prepared to explain that it had risen around 11 the night before, then go through the predictable round of queries—"Are you sure? Are you sure?"—before watching her yield to the same dread I was starting to feel.

But she just gave me an odd look. "The what?"

I laughed. "You know, that big round shiny white thing in the sky."

She gave me an even stranger look and then glanced up, warily tilting her head back and rolling her eyes as though this "moon" might be floating over her head, a Christmas play angel searching doubtfully for her halo. I laughed again, with appreciation for her faultless timing.

"But seriously," I said. "It should be there." I pointed decisively. As though she didn't quite comprehend the gesture, she looked at the tip of my finger and edged her gaze a few feet outwards before rounding back on me.

"What are you talking about, Daniel?"

"The moon! It should be out tonight and it's not."

"Are you—are you sure?" she asked in a suddenly vulnerable, tentative voice. I now interpret this last brave attempt to take me in good faith as a sign that she did, at one point, love me.

"Yes!"

"What is it?" she asked, scanning the sky because that was where I kept looking. "Some kind of nocturnal bird? Like a nighthawk?"

"Okay," I said. "Enough. I'm starting to freak out a little bit here."

She stared at me with the beginnings of the recoiling, fearful look I would grow so accustomed to. I feel for the mad now, all the crazies whose paths I crossed with blind indifference for so many years. Until you lose the endorsement of others, you don't realize how much you depend on their tacit judgment that you are sane, nor appreciate that they pass this judgment, and communicate it, with the same split-second glance.

She tried to speak. "I just…" She looked away. "I just don't understand what you're talking about."

"The moon, the damn moon! The most obvious thing in the world! The earth's satellite!"

She gushed with relief. "Oh, a satellite! Sorry! I haven't been following the news. Is it Russian? Is it going to fall?"

The tables turned. When someone you think you know suddenly reveals what is either madness or an unsuspected imbecility, it's almost gut-wrenching. I retracted my sympathy for the mad.

Then, backtracking from the whole situation, I decided I was being foolish. Helen had withdrawn into a peevish, bewildered sulk. Maybe, I thought, recognizing the tenor of her mood, she hadn't had an orgasm. Maybe her whole pretense of not understanding me was an oblique gesture of dissatisfaction, a sort of displaced revenge.

"Forget it," I said, pulling her gently to my side. She stiffened, but said nothing. It was still a beautiful night, even without the moon.

o

THE NEXT MORNING Helen was gone. I leapt out of bed and rifled through the recycling bin for the Saturday paper, which ran an astronomy column, to confirm that I was correct about the moon's phase.

This was just me being fastidious: I'm a person who sometimes loses debates over points of fact even when I'm absolutely right, and know that I'm right, because my (to me) civilized tendency is always to allow that I may be wrong. This prevents me from summoning the dogmatic tone, the rude body language, the belittling sneers, necessary to win an argument. I'm vulnerable to stupid but forceful counterattacks, and nine times out of ten the juries in these matters are swayed by them too—classmates, partygoers, dinner companions. So I just wanted to make sure that I wouldn't undermine myself in any forthcoming disputes. I was even prepared to find that I'd been mistaken, to find that the moon was new, that I simply had lost track of its cycle, in which case I would have to account for a week which seemed to have disappeared—not a pleasant prospect, but preferable to explaining the disappearance of a heavenly body. I was not prepared for a sky chart that made no mention of the moon whatsoever.

I swore at the newsroom staffer who'd bungled the chart on the one day in history when someone actually needed it. I called the paper and demanded an editor. As soon as the jaded voice answered, my resolve to stay calm evaporated.

"I'm calling about the sky charts last Saturday. You left out the moon and its phases!"

From his weary sigh, I knew this was someone who'd dealt with countless angry readers—crossword puzzlers enraged over mismatched clues, birders irate that their accidentals hadn't been reported—and loathed us all for our arid monomanias, our figmentary touchstones.

"The what?"

"I'm serious! This is serious!"

"Yeah, yeah. Listen. It was up to me we'd drop astrology altogether, so if your precious sign was missing I'm sorry, but to me it's a step in the right direction."

"Not astrology, the moon! The sky charts, the astronomy column…"

"I'll pass your complaint on, sir." He hung up.

My instinct to explain away the inexplicable was overwhelming. The editor, I reassured myself, was laughing with his pals—"I pretended I didn't know what the idiot was talking about!" My need to understand—the need, rather, for events and actions to be understandable—was it keeping me sane? Or was this impulse responsible for my madness? (Nothing, not the most durable fact, survives absolute scrutiny; everything dissolves into words, and the codependency of definitions.) I couldn't tell. Like the night before with Helen: either she was mad and I was not, or I was and she was not. How could I tell? Archimedes asked for a place to stand so that he could move the world. Let me outside of myself, I begged, just long enough to determine whether I've gone crazy.

In the mirror I saw myself trembling. A thousand possible courses of action came to me; I phoned in sick to the call center where I worked, and over the next few hours I pursued dozens of them. I was aware of my sanity as I had never been in my life. It's something you don't even know you have until you feel it going away. Then it's like—like the moon. The one that followed your car when you were a kid in the back seat. Your parents said it was tied to the fender by a long string. Except this time the string snapped and it floated away. Which is what happened while I was standing at a busy intersection, appealing ever more desperately of the people who passed:

"Do you remember the moon?"

o

SOMETIME LATER I woke up and opened my eyes. A corolla of pink daubs swam over me. They slowly resolved—and I knew the wonder Galileo must have felt when he peered at Jupiter through his telescope and spied four objects circling it — into faces, loved ones, the ones whose lives and mine were interlaced in dizzying Ptolemaic convolvuli.

A wave of relief washed over me. I must have smiled; soft reciprocal smiles rewarded me, my relief seeming to spread. I tried to speak, found my mouth fused shut. A paper cup of water was produced and I drank it gratefully.

"What a nightmare!" My voice was a croak and the tender smiles became grins.

"For all of us, dear," said my mother.

"When I was…" What? Unconscious? Comatose? I hypothesized quickly, sketched in a bike accident to explain my hospitalization, surmised that a headlight, yes, yes, one burning headlight, was the last thing I saw before my world went dark, and out of this shred of memory I'd dreamed my senseless dream of a world that had never known the moon. My parents, Helen, my doctor (not yet known as such) — they edged closer, concern replacing the previous moment's delight. "I'm okay!" I laughed, finding their intensity comical. "I remember everything, all of you, all of me. But it was weird. I dreamt there was no moon."

Suddenly my mother was quietly crying and my father was sucking in his lips, while Helen turned away in embarrassment. I groaned and closed my eyes, though not before noticing that the doctor appeared rather pleased.

o

MARCHING ME AROUND the hospital grounds, my father referred to "this business" in a workmanlike manner, a problem we would lick together as we had so many others, and he assumed I shared his view that the only obstacle in our path was the medical profession. It was painful for me to observe him; each time I alluded to my belief in the moon, he cranked his resolve to a higher level—until finally he could no longer pretend that we were making any progress, and something foundational in him collapsed. The tension left him, and he sagged and his hard eyes melted into a baffled helplessness: he'd taken it for granted that he could straighten me out, and his failure was a mortal blow. He blamed himself and concluded that for the first time in his life a crucial task was beyond his powers. Were they diminishing, or had he overestimated them all along? In short, I set off a crisis in him.

My mother, meanwhile, seemed bent on making herself as miserable as possible by insisting that we meet in the lounge. The walls were bruise-yellow with their nicotine film, the tubular metal chairs and couch were upholstered in a sort of dark brown burlap, and the room was otherwise unfurnished, save for the TV and a catatonic named George, who'd been installed a decade previously. It was explained to families who requested privacy that his presence was not considered a violation of this request. He disturbed my mother so much that I kept urging her to take a walk, but she refused, and I began to suspect that George served a purpose. She often directed cold, reproachful glances his way, looks which might otherwise have settled on me.

Her strategy for curing me involved placing the grief I was causing her on silent exhibition. Wouldn't I stop having delusions for her sake please? But when she, as my father had, confronted the unmovable object that was my belief, she too took it as her own failure, a failure of love, and left in tears with a dark parting glance at George.

Helen was reluctant to visit at all. I couldn't blame her: she had been with me when I'd gone mad. We'd been having sex moments before my madness revealed itself, and she probably wondered whether I had snapped during the act. I suppose a sultrier and less sane woman could have made seductive profit from the tale, but Helen wasn't like that. At a fundamental level she was repulsed by the entire situation.

I just wanted her—wanted anyone—to whisper that he or she remembered the moon too, and was keeping quiet until we could get a better grasp of the situation.

I was not being treated yet. Everyone agreed that in other respects I was perfectly sane, and it seemed that curing me should be easy. I had a strange belief; all they had to do was talk me out of it. But they couldn't. And there was nothing I could do to alleviate the demoralizing effect I was having on these people, which filled me with such shame that I was relieved when the burden shifted to the professionals who'd been sharpening their knives on the sidelines, certain that my loved ones would fail—specifically, to Marvin Pallister, the doctor who'd smiled when I'd come out of unconsciousness, madness in tact.

○

SOME MOONS SLICED through the night like the fins of sharks in still black oceans, leaving no more wake than the blade of a knife deboning watered silk. Others lumbered into view so heavy and pregnant that it was all our eyes could do to help them over the sky, moons we glanced up at incessantly, like faithful dogs.

○

DR MARVIN PALLISTER did not strike me as the sort of person to whom I could confidently entrust my mind.

I don't know how reliable external traits are as indicators of a man's inner being. Some would say that traits are reliable just to the extent that an interpreter is capable of reading them. In the special case of those to whom we entrust our psyches, our souls (be they priests or doctors or judges), we expect them to have exceptional insight into character—an ability to see into us, to discern something of our natures simply by observing us. If character is something that is revealed through action, then the only action these men and women need to observe us perform is *being*. When we are in the presence of these diviners we expect to sense their insight—in a level, penetrating gaze, or in the air of wisdom or gravitas they exude.

Pallister did not have this presence, this gaze, which must mean one of three things: that a man's bearing is not a valid indicator of his acumen; that it is, but I lack the means of discernment which facilitate judgments about character—I just couldn't see his wisdom; or that he never really did have any insight into me, in which case I was correct in my initial assessment of him, and mistaken in later giving him my trust.

In appearance, in outlook, in manner, he belonged in the world of objects, not of minds. He was about forty, burly, balding, with strong forearms and blunt hands. He had the unconscious habit, whenever he glimpsed my messier corners, of leaning forward with his fists clenching and unclenching: if he could just get his hands on my thoughts he'd fix them up fine. He was genial, friendly to staff and patients alike, greeting them with a smile that revealed crooked, tense teeth, in a voice that was higher than one would have expected and strained as though he'd spent too much time in taverns, shouting to be heard. His face was round, though his jaw was somewhat lumpy. The beard he later grew was so obvious an enhancement that it immediately became impossible to remember what he'd looked like without it.

He was also touchy, impatient with abstraction, uncomfortable when sitting, brusque or even rude when acknowledging greetings rather than initiating them, aggressive but given to outbreaks of lassitude and even despair, in short more volatile than one might wish one's psychiatrist to be. None of this is to suggest that he was incompetent: he was a senior member of the staff, taught at the university, had two books and a dozen articles to his credit, and proved himself quick and deft in tracing logical outcomes from my premises. It's just that he seemed to have chosen, not the wrong profession, but the wrong universe. At times he was exasperated by the very concept of mind and maybe he was here from an outraged sense of duty, to stamp out the fires of mind where they burned most raggedly.

He was a psychiatrist. Not a psychotherapist or a psychologist or, god forbid, a psychoanalyst. "We don't fight fire with fire around here. Cool water is what we use. Just the cool water of reason."

"To wash the pills down."

He bared his teeth. "Oh, a wise guy. Tell me, what's a pill but the fruit of the tree of reason? In fact a pill is reason. Precipitated in the crucibles, annealed, chelated, bound by a few inactive starches, and taken orally by those whose reason it is intended to restore."

"You're going to give me a pill so I don't remember the moon?"

"Would if I could, my friend," he said, "but I can't. So we're going to have to talk it over. Tell me about this moon of yours."

o

So BEGAN MY EXTENDED, haphazard seminar in lunar astronomy. The gaps in my knowledge embarrassed me. Sometimes I said one thing, realized later I must have been wrong, and retracted my claim, just as Pallister was about to demonstrate its inconsistency. He would tilt his head back and smile down on me. And some aspects of the moon just made no sense.

"A full moon looks enormous near the horizon," I told him once, "then seems to shrink as it rises. But if you hold an aspirin at arm's length you find it covers the moon perfectly, whether it's on the horizon or at its zenith."

Pallister jotted this down in his notebook. He didn't care about this imaginary object as such, but from his point of view every fact about it was a symptom of my disorder and a possible clue to its cure. "Why did it look bigger on the horizon?"

"Nobody quite knew. It was an illusion."

These were the moments he loved, when the eccentricity of my claims delighted him. My moon, like a character in a novel, never seemed so alive as when it behaved, against all efforts of its creator to make it consistent, inconsistently.

"What do you mean nobody knew? It wasn't just some lensing effect of the atmosphere?"

"Nope. Like I said, an illusion."

I struggled to describe eclipses. Why weren't there two eclipses every month, one when the moon passed between earth and sun, and one when the earth passed between sun and moon? Because the plane of the moon's orbit was skewed to the plane of the earth's orbit. Then why were there eclipses at all? Because sometimes they all lined up. So this must have happened at regular intervals? No. At predictable intervals, but not regular ones. Why? Why? Because! Because! Because it was where it was and not somewhere else! Why was it where it was?

And why not only did the moon fit perfectly over the sun, but also did the earth's shadow fit perfectly over the moon? Didn't that seem a bit too perfect?

It was a ridiculous investigation of the unthinkable, yet Pallister welcomed every shred of information I could dredge up.

"The first man landed on the moon in 1969."

Pallister's eyebrows rose. "Men on the moon? How did they get there?"

"On rockets. Apollos."

"Apollos? We've got those."

"Big white things?"

"Exactly." It pleased us to agree, when we could. "And were people excited about these moon landings? Scared? Did they expect to find life? Or…" He leafed back through his notes until he found the reference he sought. "Cheese?"

"It was a major event, a milestone. People marked their lives by it." I refused to take responsibility for the legends that had grown up around the moon or to be embarrassed by them. "Though some people thought it was all a hoax, filmed in a buried TV studio, maybe by Stanley Kubrick."

"Did those people believe there was no such thing as the moon? Or just that men never really landed on it?"

"They were paranoid conspiracy theorists."

"And did the moon attract paranoid conspiracy theorists in general?" he asked after a long silence.

But he was perplexed and fascinated by my claim that the moon's cycle was twenty-eight days. "Twenty-eight? But that's—that's the menstrual cycle."

"Yes. Yes, I know."

"Was there a causal link? Do you believe the moon influenced menstruation? Or that menstrual cycles governed the moon?"

I could see where this was leading. From his perspective it was terribly significant, a sign that my delusion might spring from a primitive sexual phobia. He returned to this often, seeing it as a weak point in my argument. Moon after moon waxed to a fullness which endured thirty hours; thirty hours is how long an ovum is in the state of receptivity in which it can be fertilized. Then the bloody black walls in which it was embedded dissolved and washed the wasted egg from its sky.

"Why twenty-eight days?" Pallister demanded again and again. I didn't know; I don't know; I fell back to my last line of defence.

"That's just the way it was."

He insisted that I confess my aversion to blood, and whenever I denied this (never deny anything too vehemently to a psychiatrist), he would sit back, lace his fingers together, and smile as though he'd won the point. "Of course you deny it. That's because you dispatched your revulsion so successfully. You imagined a 'moon' and then banished it. Now you want to know where this moon is which you remember so well, and whose disappearance has awakened such torment and anxiety in you. Where'd the moon go? Simple. It's in the same place your horror of blood is."

"The same side always faced the earth," I explained another day. "There was a dark side we could never see."

"Why? Didn't it rotate?"

"Think! If it didn't rotate, we *would* see the whole surface, a slightly different portion each night."

He stared into middle distance, concentrating furiously. "Oh, yeah," he agreed, relaxing when he'd modelled this. "But then why did only one side show?"

Sometimes I hated the arbitrary thing. Sometimes I wished he could cure me. "Because," I said, "the time the moon took to rotate on its axis was identical to the time it took to orbit once around the earth."

He grinned and started writing. "Beautiful," he said under his breath, shaking his head with admiration. "The dark side remains ever hidden," he said, reciting aloud as he wrote. "You're lucky I'm not a Jungian."

o

THESE DISCUSSIONS, despite our flare-ups, were civilized and leisurely, marked by sincere efforts to understand one another. Pallister complimented me on my lucidity and declared that I was passably sane in every respect save my belief in this object. I affirmed in turn that reality was to my satisfaction in all observable matters save those relating to the absence of same. But the very normalcy of things was making me suspicious.

After much begging on my part, Pallister gave me permission to visit the hospital's library. This was a huge privilege in an institution which forbade some of its inmates from reading at all (a ban which would surely drive them mad if they weren't already). I wanted to search for non-scientific and incidental lunar references, and I started confidently in that most moon-soaked of classifications—Poetry—and emerged from it shaken. All of the usual poems were there, but none mentioned the moon, not one.

Undaunted, I racked my memory for more oblique moon references. This was just me being paranoid and desperate, thinking that, okay, maybe They (who?!) could censor all the obvious mentions of the moon, but that I could outsmart Them. So, for example, I remembered that in the 14th century Pope Clement VI had suffered from "brain fever." His surgeons, intending to saw open his skull to relieve the pressure, postponed the planned trepanation for three nights *because the moon was full*, which would cause the cranial meninges to swell. When I found this account in the history of medicine section, I found that nothing had changed—except the swelling was now attributed to the tides. But what caused the tides and how had life even evolved without them?

For weeks I pursued similar lines of inquiry, and all I found out was that history had unfolded in this moonless world exactly as I remembered it had in the one with a moon. None of it made any more sense than the absence of the moon itself.

Pallister must have been thinking along the same line.

"Listen, I'm having trouble," he said one day. "Something's out of whack. Pardon me for bringing sci-fi into it, but it's the only way I can get my hands on the problem. There's a sub-genre of stories called alternate histories. The author imagines that something in the past occurred differently, the Nazis won the war for example."

"They didn't? So how do I explain you?"

He ignored me. "Or as another example, you start reading and you're plunged into a present which is strangely different: a phenomenally advanced society, but one in which everything is steam-driven—steam technology has been miniaturized, 600-mile-an-hour steam trains connect London to Rome—and the reader's enjoyment derives from trying to think backwards and figure out what happened differently in the past to set history on this alternate track. So what I'm getting at…"

I knew what he was getting at and I didn't have an explanation. I tried to stall. "Why was everything run by steam?"

"Hmm? Oh, because electricity was never harnessed. But the point…"

I held up my hand. "Hang on, hang on. Why not?"

An anguished, incredulous expression crossed his face, but he suppressed his exasperation, manfully shouldering the blame for this digression.

"Electricity was never harnessed because Catholic church bans on research that was deemed to tamper with God's mysteries forced Robert Maxwell off his course as a physicist into a brilliant career as a steam-engine researcher instead."

"But Maxwell—wasn't he Scottish? A Protestant? Why would he care about the Church?"

"That's the twist!" He was getting excited despite himself. "You see, the deeper cause was that the Reformation never happened! Luther died before he could nail his page to the doors, maybe he was killed, I can't quite remember."

"So let me get this straight—no Luther means no Reformation means no scientific revolution? That's a bit inflammatory towards Catholicism, isn't it?"

"The point," he nearly shouted; hearing his own voice, he took a breath and pulled his shoulders back, before continuing in a more level tone, "is that if there was never such a thing as this moon of yours, which seems to have been so important, history should have convulsed in some way, a big way, yet you say this world, this parallel strand of reality, is identical to the strand that contained a moon. That doesn't make much sense, does it? The whole point of alternate histories as an intellectual exercise is to explore the avalanche of changes that even the slightest alteration to the past sets off."

"Well, I'm sorry, but if reality and cause and effect don't obey the same laws that they do in a Kingsley Amis novel, maybe the problem is Kingsley Amis, not reality."

This time he did shout. "You know what I mean!"

"Yes," I confessed, sagging into my chair.

o

ALL THOSE ANCIENT SIEGES hastened or delayed by moonlight had played out the same way without a moon. The apparent fact that life had not been altered by the elimination of so enormous an element suggested that the interpretation of events as endlessly complex interactions of cause and effect was comforting nonsense: a relentless plan was being imposed, and whether the moon was in the sky or not didn't matter a bit.

The only rational explanation? God had watched the world unfurl, decided the moon was flawed, reversed history, killed the silver child, overdubbed all reference to it, and fast-forwarded back to the present. And why not? It was His game. If He wanted to take back a move, it was His right. Why He should have done so, and why I and only I had noticed, were not for me to know.

o

YET I'D NOTICED that people reacted to my mention of the moon, not as though I were speaking gibberish, but with brow-furrowed puzzlement, as though I were using a vaguely familiar word in an unfamiliar way. And during my reading I had found occasional, dim mentions of *his moone* or a *moone devotion*, though these never referred to an actual object. So I expected to find it defined, probably as an archaic astronomical term, since discarded, for the satellites of the other planets (which were now simply called satellites), and that's what the first few dictionaries said. But when I obtained Brewer's *Dictionary of Phrase and Fable* on an interlibrary loan, I was shocked: the entry for moon ran a full column, and the ancient usages left me reeling.

It meant absence. It meant desire. It meant permanence; but impermanence too. On and on it went. The word "moon" was now a forgotten term meaning everything which the moon I remember had ever been taken as a symbol for. It haunted, it memorialized, it illuminated, it occluded; it had so many meanings that it was in effect indefinable, like beauty.

I tried to make sense of this. An object had vanished, and with that object had gone the primary meaning of the word that named it; but the word remained, and all the object's symbolic connotations had rushed in, filling the vacuum. The signifier had outlasted its referent, and had become, by default, a referent itself for a swarm of allusive signifiers.

Would it be possible for me to demonstrate that the moon

had existed by establishing that only an object fitting my description of it could have satisfied each and every one of the faint meanings now given to the word? And if there really was a force which had eliminated the moon from existence, yet left a ghostly residue in the language, could this force eliminate other objects? Had the same thing in fact happened already? Had our most nebulous words originally been attached to objects as plain to the eye as the moon? Had there once been a love, a freedom, a soul, a faith? A god? Did our dutiful calendars once record their slotted cycles through the night? Had I stumbled across evidence of a process by which the objects so named were made to vanish, the memory that they had ever existed being confined to a few pathetic individuals who were deemed mad by the majority, a majority whose amnesia was a vital part of the process? Were Things—the moon, the love, the soul—no longer necessary once they'd attracted a critical mass of symbolic meaning? When saturated with reference could they be annulled?

Or did our compulsion to attach symbolic significance to Things cause them to fade and vanish?

o

ONE NIGHT A THUNDERSTORM broke around 2 AM. I lay in bed with the window open, listening, trying to categorize thunders. When I was in high school one of my friends had an old analog synthesizer that let you sculpt the shape of each note by calibrating qualities called attack, sustain, decay, and release. Whoever programmed the thunder was pounding away on a keyboard with similar features. Sometimes a low rumble began in the distance and overlapping volleys advanced, awakening the expectation of a crescendo which never came, attack yielding to decay seamlessly. Then triple warheads detonated overhead and the reverberations they unloosed slapped back and forth against the walls of their holding tank until the staggered waves became hopelessly tangled and they died off abruptly, in the backwash of their own interference patterns. Rain all the while hissed like the background static of radiation that circumscribes the universe.

Adrift in the room with my eyes closed I indulged this conceit and imagined I was scanning deep space, listening to a radio telescope, and that each burst of thunder was the signature print of another distant astral body swimming briefly through my focus. The conceit took root and soon it really felt as though space, not time, separated the thunderclaps, and I seemed to be spinning slowly on my axis through the night. Then my mind, cluttered with the flotsam of three months of fanatical research, tossed up the word "borborygmy," the scientific term for stomach rumbling, and my imagination handled the descent from the heavens deftly and I was a foetus in its womb, diverted by the mysterious commotions beyond the edges of my world as I floated in a private sea; and then I was, less happily, a lump of something being digested, and the thunder was peristalsis and the hissing rain was gastric acid corroding my substance as the gut that contained me racked and heaved.

Oddly enough this proved to be the most comforting image of them all, because a partial dissolution of self accompanied it, as though, despite the baseness of my starting place, I'd nonetheless entered a transcendental state, and the digestive process was nothing less than my absorption by universal Being.

But in the morning, though that sense of diffusion remained, gone was its comforting emotional tone, and my mood was already bleak when I looked outside and saw to my shock that the rain had battered the trees bare. So much time had passed since my admission to the hospital, but it was only the spectacle of the trees stripped and their ransacked leaves that brought me face to face with the waste I'd made of it. Half a year, gone.

I gathered the hundreds of pages of notes I'd made in my delineation of the moon's erasure and stuffed them into a drawer in the metal desk. I slid it shut on its quiet runners and considered the case closed.

I could not let go of my belief in the moon, but I was ready to concede defeat and live out the balance of a life stunted by incomprehension. Which may have been all I ever expected of life in the first place. For a few days I barely left my room. Nobody took much notice, and their indifference to me accurately reflected my own. Eventually, however, Pallister registered my seclusion. There was a knock on the door, and he entered, with uncharacteristic hesitation.

"I have good news," I told him. "I've given up. I don't believe I can explain my delusions. So I renounce them."

Oddly, he wasn't pleased. He probed for weaknesses or inconsistencies in my purported renunciation, much as he had searched for flaws in the logic of the delusion, and after a time he sat back and settled into a pensive silence. He regarded me with a curious expression and kept clicking a pencil up and down between his teeth.

"I don't believe you," he said at last.

"Fine. Don't."

"I think you're fooling yourself. You're exhausted from your research and maybe the absurdity of your line of thinking is finally clear to you. You failed at an impossible task. Now you want to lick your wounds. Understandable. Right now you don't have the energy to confront your delusion so you're trying to ignore it. But I can't accept that you're cured and I know you don't either."

"You're just pissed off at me for curing myself."

He laughed. "Don't worry about me. If you really do cure yourself I'll get the credit for initiating this, hmm, innovative self-directed approach to therapy shall we call it? The whole point of which is that neither of us will understand your delusion until we identify the cognitive malfunction that triggered it. In giving you freedom to go off on these chases, I've been banking that some inaccessible part of your mind will lead you to the answer. From what you're telling me, you haven't found it yet. So you're copping out."

"Yes. I'm copping out."

"Well then." He stood. "Let me know when you're ready to cop in again."

o

BRASH YOUNG CRESCENTS polished to perfection and edged to die-cut sharpness popped from nowhere into blue afternoon skies—look at me!—gauche, addle-brained debutantes, who yet turned our sardonic smiles to wistful expressions of surrender, we who were not so beautiful that we could sail through our silliest blunders.

o

FOR A FEW DAYS I tried not to believe anything at all. But incomprehension is an intolerable state. Explanations rushed in to fill the void.

In the Vedanta, the moon ferried souls from this realm to a higher one, where the soul is liberated from desire. If this story were true, what would it mean that the moon had vanished?

It would mean there were no more souls left.

They'd all been rescued from our false world of matter; any persons remaining were, it followed, without soul. But

I thought of the Fall of Saigon, footage of the last American choppers rising from the embassy roof with desperate friendlies clinging to the undercarriage: somebody is always left behind in these evacuation scenarios, and in this case it was me. The torment I felt at the moon's disappearance wasn't shared by anyone else for the simple reason that they were mere brutes of clay who had never seen the moon in the first place, because they'd never had souls trapped inside them, like the soul which had seen the moon through my eyes.

Pallister paid little attention to me when I outlined my new explanation.

"Of course you won't believe me," I said. "You don't have a soul."

For a few weeks the idea consoled me in a miserably adolescent sort of way. I indulged in a moody critique of the modern world, showing that it was made and populated by beings without soul. I proved further that a decline in the world's quotient of the soulful was the most glaring trend in human history. Scoop by scoop the moon had emptied Earth of the holy, until there was none left, and the scoop could be taken off its hook in the sky and shoved to the back of a drawer. Pallister didn't say much to refute my new hypothesis, confident that its sterility would wear me down, and he was right: soon I was back in the library, researching madly. Pallister caught sight of me across the room and grinned. I ignored him.

A vivid, disorienting dream had inspired the renewal of

my quest to understand. Something about trying to read a book whose words and lines kept dissolving into pixelated streams—except every so often I'd catch a glimpse of a phrase which suggested these lines bore an answer I was desperate to find.

The dream expelled me. In the first dazed seconds of consciousness I thought that my expulsion was a terrible inadvertence and tried to sleep my way back into it. I moved through the rest of the day oblivious to my world, concentrating on the dream as though I were carrying a spoonful of water which must not spill, aware that any element which I did not refresh every few seconds was in danger of vanishing, and that once it was gone I wouldn't even remember that it had existed.

I eventually realized that the key to the dream was the perceptual disability I suffered in it. I recalled Descartes' demon of doubt, that undetectable agent of subversion who interpolated false images between world and mind. What if a lesser demon, a lunar specialist, had set up a blockade, confiscating every item of sensory input related to the moon and sending a counterfeit through in its place? Could I translate that vivid phantom into coherent scientific terms? How would Descartes have limned his fiend if he'd had MRI scans at hand? I staked out a table in the hospital library.

This time its resources were more than adequate to my task, for my goals were in perfect harmony with those of the institution itself, as though incarceration within its walls had imbued me with its mission. Soon I'd built a rampart of texts and monographs and offprints on neurophysiology. I wasn't allowed to take them from the library and I had to surrender them to any staff who requisitioned them. Several times a week one doctor or another hove towards my table and paused to regard me with a generally somewhat nauseous look, before asking for the book they needed. I understood their discomfort; it's disquieting to observe someone you consider mad reading your books and scribbling feverish notes. *Am I like that* you wonder.

The passage of time is nowhere more painless than in the study, which is why scholarship is dangerous. Pain is our best defence against harm and when we are etherized by an obsession we are at our most vulnerable. Time can tear chunks from your life, feast on your living flesh while you're numbed by dreams of reason.

Pallister, initially so pleased by my renewed devotion, became suspicious and meddlesome. He would pick through the books on my table and query me in a sharp tone on minutiae of neural functioning. Like a medical espionage agent he tried to tease out the substance of my research, but I resisted.

After months of exhaustive study, I was finally ready. I knocked on his door.

"Maybe the problem is with me, not the moon, and has been all along," I announced. He was pleased as men are when they think you've come around to their way of thinking, and I paused to extend this moment before continuing. "Maybe the moon never vanished at all. Maybe the moon is still there but I can't see it. Maybe every time I ask you where it went, you say *it's right there*. But my brain is jammed and I think you're saying *there's no such thing*. Maybe my mind deletes every reference to the moon, written or verbal, pictorial or poetic."

As I spoke, an expression spread across Pallister's face which was almost one of rapture, as though he'd placed all his bets on me and I was paying off with more madness than he'd dared to dream of. "Nod if you understand what I'm saying." He nodded. "Nod again if I'm right." He shook his head. "Maybe you just nodded, but I saw you shake your head."

"That is truly crazy. That is so goddamn crazy it's almost brilliant."

I admitted that my new hypothesis defied belief. I could understand how someone might hallucinate the moon's absence from the night sky, once or even repeatedly. But could I really censor every written or spoken reference to it—and then replace these references with coherent substitutes? I would, for one thing, need a measure of prescience. Say I was reading about a fisherman who set out in his dory before dawn under the light of a waning half-moon. There would be no reason for me to expect in advance that the moon was about to appear, yet the mechanism of my insanity was such that it moved one or two sentences ahead of me, erasing references to the moon and replacing them with cogent and contextually apt phrases that made no mention of the white shiny thing in the sky.

But it was possible. I learned that visual data proceeds to several areas of the brain. Vision is a distributed process, and first among the regions involved is a subcortical cluster called the amygdala, which is also a key regulator of emotions. The interval between the arrival of visual data at the amygdala, and our conscious awareness of what we are seeing, is a matter of split seconds, but sometimes, when our eyes have spotted something that provokes an intense response, we react to the stimulus before we are aware that we have seen it. If we stumble upon a bloody body, for example, the amygdala, panicking, may trigger a jolt of adrenaline, with the result that we feel fear before we've even finished processing the visual data; and then we attribute quasi-supernatural powers to ourselves, because it seems in retrospect that we reacted to blood before we saw it.

But a reaction consisting of the release of adrenaline is one thing; it's quite another for the amygdala to intercept moon-related input, then access the cerebral cortex, then suppress the original data, and then replace it with an equally coherent statement, but one which would only make sense in a world that had never known the moon. Was I to believe that my brain could rewrite Proposition 66 of the *Principia* with a credible alternative, and do so in a millisecond, when it would have taken me weeks of arduous work in a research library to accomplish this consciously? This seemed unlikely; but the key was that the credible alternative only had to fool one person: me. So maybe, just maybe, it was possible.

That our brains were wired so that we could react without thinking, without knowing what we were reacting to, was an admirable bit of evolutionary self-defence. Sometimes the body can't risk letting the vacillating, rationalizing mind mess things up. Perhaps, then, it was literally a matter of life and death that I should suddenly go blind to the moon. Maybe it was vital to my survival that I neither see it, nor see any reference to it, nor hear anybody refer to it or acknowledge that it existed. Or, to narrow the parameters, perhaps there had been a single moment of crisis when it had been crucial to obliterate the moon, and though the crisis had passed the short-circuit remained in place.

Granting, for the sake of argument, that it was indeed possible for my brain to censor book and sky, all I needed was to answer one question: why on earth would it ever be vital to a man's survival that he not see the moon? Why would it have mattered that I find no scrap of evidence for its existence, even as I remembered it so well? What could have induced this lunar trauma?

Was I a werewolf, one who'd been cured by extensive deep-brain therapy, the cost being my delusion that the moon was gone? An astronaut whose mission had ended in disaster so horrific that I could not admit the moon's actuality?

Or had something horrific occurred while I happened to be watching the moon, and in my suppression of memories of the horror had I suppressed the moon too? So that now if I were to see the moon a flood of unbearable recollections would also be released? The moon was associated with a terror; to protect myself from the memories of the terror, I'd projected these memories, sent them to the moon, then expunged the moon from existence.

o

ONCE HE GRASPED my theorem in its entirety, Pallister became frustrated. He said I was correct in thinking that my delusional state may have been induced by some kind of traumatic episode. "But you're missing one point: there is no frigging moon!"

After a few days of fruitless debate he summoned me to his office. I walked in, and found my father hunched in a chair. My heart sank. This was unfair.

Pallister smiled and clapped my shoulder. "Here he is, Mr. Hale, still crazy after all these years but otherwise brilliant as ever. He has a new theory. Why don't you explain it, Daniel?"

I hadn't seen my father in months. He seemed to have aged at least a decade. I felt so responsible for his state that I wanted to run out the door. But I stayed. We spoke for a few minutes about normal things; he was still phoning my employer every week, fighting on my behalf for the job that he considered beneath me. Then he asked me, then ordered me, when I refused, to explain my theory. When I was finished, he looked at me with hopeless but shielded eyes, as though he and my mother had vowed that I was not going to hurt them any more than I already had.

"Doctor Pallister mentioned that you'd taken a downturn," he finally said, "but he didn't specify. Now you believe this moon thing is there, even though you can't see it? Is that what you're trying to tell me?"

"I'm assuming you just said something to the effect that 'of course the moon's still there—where could it have gone? Where could it possibly have gone?' Is that what you said, dad?"

He hesitated for a long time, as though considering whether to play along, to join me in the solitude of my madness for an hour or two. I guess he couldn't see the point. "No," he whispered.

"Was that a 'yes' dad?" I asked.

"No, son. No, it wasn't."

o

NOT LONG AFTER my father's visit, I overheard the end of a conversation between Pallister and another doctor. They weren't speaking loudly, but the painted cinderblock walls of the corridors sustained their voices.

"But, what, two years now Marvin? Be reasonable."

"Your point is taken. He could, under proper supervision,

manage in a less intensive setting. But the opportunity…"

The other doctor interrupted gently. "We're going to need that room some day, Marvin. You know that."

There was silence. I pictured Pallister chewing this suggestion over, letting the words resonate until they seemed to be little more than a witless statement of the obvious. The other man sighed.

"Okay," he conceded, "there's no pressing need. But when that day arrives…"

A chair scraped on the floor and I fled to my room before anyone could catch me listening in.

I sat on my bed and pondered. I couldn't decide whether I should be pleased that Pallister advocated continuing treatment, or angry that he wouldn't release me. One thing was certain, though: everyone, me, Pallister, the staff, my parents, had been demoralized by my latest hypothesis. I seemed to be madder than ever.

○

THEN I HAD an illumination at my darkest moment. I had overlooked something.

I returned to my early speculation that the lingering abstract meanings of "moon" were evidence that it had disappeared, and my extrapolation that other "things"—the love, the faith, the soul, the god—had already vanished. Maybe I had it backwards; maybe these things hadn't yet appeared.

Consider the discoveries of atomic physics: when scientists divine new particles, they are in fact inferring their existence from the effects these particles have. Nobody has ever seen a neutrino; ghostly traces, unpredicted behaviors, and circumstantial evidence slowly accrete, until a threshold is passed and physicists declare with some confidence that a certain subset of observations can be accounted for if one postulates the existence of an atom, an electron, a lepton, a nuon. Do other things pass through this cycle? Before something is born into our awareness does it make its presence felt, in subtle stirrings which a few delicate, impressionable instruments or persons (like me) sense on our side of the barrier; and when it flees does it leave behind a cloud of allusions and impressions and dreams? Things quickened, things emerged, things vanished.

Maybe there had never been a moon; everyone who said so was right. But there would be—soon. It was coming. Its approach had registered ambiguously over the millennia, in myths and visions and dreams, but now it was close, close enough that at least one unfortunate sensitive fool, as finely tuned as an x-ray screen in a particle accelerator, could already describe it, had already been so impressed by it that he believed his premonitions were memories.

How I suddenly longed for the moon to be born. If the mobs didn't murder me for sorcery they would have to hail me as a prophet. I could see it rising for the first time—ever—so vividly in my imagination that I spent every night at my window, staring into the starry sky. I succumbed to the mystery. I no longer cared whether I would ever understand it.

My doctor seemed to wax as I waned. I saw much less of him now. He'd risen above mere treatment of a patient: he had published an article on "Hale–Pallister's Lunacy" and now he had a whole syndrome to tackle. There was no more mention of discharging me to free up a room. Everyone was content to keep me around like a venerated senior partner, or like Bartleby the scrivener in Melville's story.

Pallister did drop in for longer visits every once in a while. He'd grown his beard by now, the one that suited him so well and made it impossible to remember him without it. He pulsed with energy and threw off that light of ambition which draws people out from their shadows. He let me in on a secret: he'd been dabbling in forensic psychopathology. He'd made some posthumous diagnoses of Hale–Pallister's Lunacy. Milton, Chaucer, Shakespeare himself, all had shown signs of a low-grade affliction. I recognized the impulse, the need some medical men had to trump literary critics and art historians, soft thinkers with empirically groundless beliefs in such nonsense as imagination. When I hear the word "creative" I reach for my DSM and all that.

"Look Daniel," he said, in an apologetic tone, possibly sensing my unspoken hostility. "I can see now that I was hard on you sometimes."

"You believe that there really might have been a moon?"

He laughed, caught himself, and tamped his laughter down into a good-natured chuckle. "No, no, not at all. But I believe that other people in the past might have believed in it. I was wondering if you still have that stash of research."

Glory awaited him. He hadn't just discovered a new mental ailment; he'd unearthed a delusion centuries of medicine had overlooked. He wasn't just trumping his contemporaries: he was outdoing the past giants themselves. Now he needed a few names. I felt like a witness in the McCarthy trials, but I decided that in the long run it might help me. At the moment I was an isolated oddity of no real interest, but if Pallister was out there in the world promoting his discovery (and himself), there was always hope that Hale–Pallister's Lunacy would become a common template for madness, like the Bonaparte complex.

Maybe everyone would catch it. And that's when the moon would come. Such are the consolations of the mad.

I rose and trudged to the desk. The steel drawer squealed when I opened it. I clawed out a ragged pile of papers, the notes I'd made when I was frenetically searching through recorded history for allusions or references to the moon.

"These are the notes. There are two categories. Some quotations are the same as I remember them from the time before the moon disappeared. And some passages have changed, to omit the moon." There were hundreds of pages, covered with my tiny handwriting. "Of course, if there really is a moon..."

Pallister let out an impatient huff. His eyes had latched on to my trove of papers. "Yes yes yes."

"If there really is a moon," I repeated, patiently and slowly, enacting my spent fury the only way left to me, through ponderous recapitulation of my delusional analyses of delusion, "and if my hypothesis is true—that my unconscious is replacing occurrences of the moon with sterilized substitutes—then the so-called altered passages don't exist in any book, don't exist anywhere but in my head." Deciphering my bibliographic shorthand, not to mention my handwriting—never mind figuring out what the hell I meant—would take him months. Or one of his graduate students. I passed the stack to him. He started leafing through the pages.

"Thank you," he mumbled. "Thank you." He drifted towards the door, absorbed.

"Don't photocopy them. I wrote them in that special ink that vanishes if you try."

"Okay, sure. I'll copy them out by hand," he said, missing my joke.

o

I HAVEN'T SEEN HIM since, not in person, though once when I was passing through the lounge his face leapt out at me from the TV. George, the dilapidated hebephrenic, sat on the couch. His permanently stupefied expression suited him to the role of daytime talk-show addict; it was almost possible, when he was in the proximity of a television, to believe he was normal. Never mind that the volume was muted. On the screen, Pallister babbled and bounced in his seat. He had a new pair of gold-rimmed glasses, and with his beard neatly trimmed and his well-tailored clothes, his alert eyes, his ready smile (he'd straightened his teeth too), he was the picture of psychiatric humanity, a middle-weight Pavarotti who might burst into tears or song at any moment. I was certain he was talking about me. I sat down beside George.

"Hey George," I soothed. "You good?" He had the remote locked in his hand. The orderlies sometimes placed it there in one of those gestures of empowerment. "I'm going to turn it up a bit." I started to straighten his rigid fingers one by one. "Let's find out what he's saying."

But I was too late. All I got to hear was a wave of artificially sweetened applause before the host cut to a commercial.

It wasn't hard to guess why a psychiatrist was on the talk show circuit. Television demands occasions; madness is continual: my doctor was not just chatting randomly about his profession. Something had *happened*. The very next day my suspicion was confirmed.

As soon as I saw the book, lying on the taut, starchy sheet of my bed, I knew what it was. The drab grey card cover, the dull, plain type: a galley proof. My capacity for emotion had dwindled so much that I was surprised by the quick thrum of grief this provoked. Long, long ago, when I thought I would be a writer, I sometimes let myself visualize the moment when the galleys of my first book arrived for correction. Torn between the urge to be published, and the fear of exposure, I reasoned that having to proof my own soon-to-be-released book would be the one perfect instance in the entire process of becoming an author: I would bask in the conferral of legitimacy, before the deluge of scorn or indifference broke. Even during my first few months in this institution I'd occasionally consoled myself with the thought that when I, or the world, recovered the proper beliefs about the moon, I would write about my experience. Later, when I'd been drained by my plight, I abandoned that hope too.

It was all academic now that I had the galleys of the very book I would have written in my hand: *The Man Who Remembered the Moon*.

I tried to start at the beginning and read straight through, but soon gave in to the temptation to flip around, looking for parts about me. You'd think that wouldn't be too hard, in that I was the subject, I was *The Man*. But everywhere I found myself I found Pallister too.

"Though he was born ten years after me he seemed much younger, and even when I compare myself as I was at thirty to this curiously unsuccessful man the gulf between us is wide. It's not that I claim to be, or have been, outrageously triumphant; but at his age I was already deeply and fruitfully enmeshed in the matrices of social increase. I had responsibilities and obligations to persons and to institutions. My fulfillment of these, and let me stress at once that I often struggled, set other chains of action into motion, some of which looped back to me in the form of reward.

"By contrast Daniel has stepped lightly through his life, and were it not for a rather alarming debt load, his name might not register at all in a deep search through societal circuitry. I can't deny that elements of both envy, and of the repugnance we of the productive classes sometimes feel towards those others who are held aloft by the convection currents our labors emit, occasionally intruded upon my evaluations of this gifted underachiever. One does not allow such personal feelings to infect the quality of treatment, but nor can one pretend that they haven't arisen—the human instrument has registered them and it would be unscientific to factor them out entirely."

It's unnerving to read about yourself. As I progressed I noticed that I was growing irritated, and then troubled, by my own insubstantiality. That's not me! I protested, but what I really meant was *that's not anybody*. I found it harder and harder to feel a sense of the person by whose name these traits and statements and actions were grouped. A sequence of acts and utterances had their origin in "Daniel Hale," to whom was attributed an appearance and a history which jibed with these acts and utterances, and everything met certain standards for consistency—yet, to me, it signified nothing. I eluded my own grasp. I barely seemed real. Had Pallister failed to transplant my essence into prose? Or was it just that, the essence in this case being my own, I was encountering the deeper impossibility of such transplant? Would I have been satisfied by his portrait if it had been of anyone but me? Would anyone but me, reading this portrait, be dissatisfied?

Or did I simply have no essence?

Equally frustrating was Pallister's inability to keep himself off the page. I grant that he was justified to an extent in writing about himself—the book was about his treatment of me, and we were intertwined. But after a while it seemed that I only existed as a pretext for him to display his wit, wisdom, or compassion. Not to mention that he'd attributed many of my best lines to himself. I found myself gritting my teeth, and I tried to stay calm by reminding myself that this was a hazard of the genre: the shrinks have been stealing the light from their subjects ever since Freud.

I set the book down on my bed to ponder these questions, and as I did so I became aware of an uncanny silence. The hours had whispered past while I was engrossed in Pallister's story. Now it was dusk and the light filtering into my room through the window was dim and granular. But I heard none of the commotion that usually arose at this time of day, when thralls of the sundry dementias tended to anxiety and agitation, when muffled queries and orders burst through the PA as the night shift replaced the day, when creaky food carts clattered through the halls. For that matter, where was my dinner? The obvious explanation was that it was later than I thought; absorbed in my reading, I hadn't noticed the usual noises. Sometimes when I was young and immersed in a novel my mother had to call me five or six times before I heard her. I wasn't quite convinced that this was the case now: I had no fondness for obvious explanations. I resolved to investigate. But first I wanted to skip ahead to the conclusion of Pallister's book.

I was hoping, irrationally, that Pallister would unveil a brilliant solution to the entire gloomy conundrum, one he had mischievously withheld from me, and that the truth, revealed here, would save me. Wouldn't that make for good ad copy: read the book that cured the man the book is about when he read it! But there was nothing especially new. He ran through various hypotheses, some of them his, some mine, some (the ones he refuted most savagely) offered by colleagues and rivals, then settled for the conservative diagnosis of "a delusional world-state—a *parergon*—unusual in the complexity and rigor of its upkeep," but from which we ultimately learn very little, "fascinating though it may be."

That should have been the end. But the story continued. This, I thought, would be the sad part, the part about me in my room, fastened to the window, waiting for the moon. We all wonder about our futures, and sketch out fates and outcomes, some good and some bad, but I'm certain that few of us foresee ourselves as the unhappy ending of another man's book.

Wearily, I turned the page...

"Or did I imagine the man who remembered the moon?

"Maybe I'm an inmate in the institution I believe I run, tending to an imaginary patient in an empty room, which my custodians allow me to believe is the home of this man with his supposed delusion. But I see a photo on books, and the face matches the one I've observed in mirrors, and the name is one I answer to: ergo I really must be, or have been, a doctor. But maybe I did not observe the proper measures of professional hygiene, and fell victim to psychical contagion; now my fantasies are indulged, in deference to my past position or, less happily (maybe I was unpopular), with the goal of extracting the utmost revenge against me. I am well treated here, shuffling off to this empty room to meet with my insubstantial patient, but this very kindness may be cruelty. Clearly I need help. By comparison to me, the man who remembered the moon is but lightly touched, this madman I imagine. He suffers a first-order false belief: the belief that there was once a thing called a moon, which disappeared and sucked the evidence that it had ever existed into the black hole of its absence. Whereas I had to imagine him to negate the moon: he is the fiction who generated a moon—a moon I refuted. By believing that he is real, I believe the moon is not. Have I imagined him as a mechanism to eliminate the moon? Maybe there is a moon; maybe it's the man who remembered it who isn't real.

"I believe now that I effaced the moon by accident. I expelled

'Daniel'—that is, I created an alter personality named Daniel who embodied a set of traits I wished to dissociate from myself, as well as a second set of traits which I felt I had lost. I loathed his inexcusable underachievement, his weakness of will, his lax attitude towards life, his preoccupation with the abstract and the theoretical, even as I envied his cleverness, his quickness, and his facility with abstraction. What would have been merely a routine case of Dissociative Personality Disorder was complicated, though, by the fact that Daniel took the moon when I expelled him. Which was all for the best: without the conflict between 'us' (myself, and my alter) over the alleged moon (which I didn't believe existed), I would have happily accepted my dissociative state, and 'we' would have collaborated in living my mad contented life. Or, equally possible, we would never have become aware of one another at all.

"Now, with my healing all but complete, we can see that madness is not always without its own odd merit. The very traits which I envied in him—and in which I believed myself deficient—were, of course, aspects of me. I was the clever one! I was the quick one! I was the one with a facility for theory! My psyche, by splitting these abilities off into another personality, forced me to reclaim them; I can no longer doubt myself, having seen my talents on such visible display.

"All that remains now is for the evening to come, and it will come soon, when I open the door to the room where I have enjoyed so many hours of byplay with this gifted purveyor of absurdities, and find it empty. Empty. I note, however, that an odd, silvery light is powdered upon the sheets of the neatly made bed. And this book lies open upon it. I step to the window and gaze up and see it: the moon.

"The moon. Just as he remembered it."

Shining in an empty room.

THE ONE ABOUT THE BALLARD FANATIC

LATER, AS BLOOD THICKENS on the woven jute rug in Gennison's study, I wonder how we got on to Ballard in the first place.

I was nursing a pint of stout at a pub in Hampstead. Behind the bar, bottles glittered like gaudy cathedral saints in a common alcove; above them, a bank of silent televisions, each tuned to a different satellite news channel. The Secretary-General of the UN kept popping up as though he were trying to coax me into a game of peek-a-boo. I didn't want to play, and I returned my attention to the rapture of beige bubbles ascending the sides of my glass.

Then someone a few seats to my right snorted and mumbled "Jackpot." I glanced over to see a middle aged man tucking into a basket of chips. He sensed my attention and nodded towards the televisions.

The news cycles had briefly synchronized. All six screens were showing identical footage of a helicopter hovering over a bulbous water tank on rickety stilts, rising a hundred feet from a drab prairie that might have been Kansas or Kazakhstan. Dangling at the end of a thread extruded from the chopper's belly was a tiny knot of flailing limbs. Zoom: a geared-up trooper holding the boy he'd just plucked to safety. America then. They're the sort that care.

The barkeep was watching too.

"He's right, luv," I said to her. "It's come up all helis." I pushed my glass forward. "Pay out."

"Fat chance," she said, and stalked to the other end of the bar.

The fellow and I exchanged a wry glance, and then we both watched the stations slide out of synch, their momentary convergence as transient as the fleeting communion he and I had just shared.

WHEN I REGAIN consciousness, I'm aware of nothing but a repetitive thud in my left ear, drumming out through an oceanic swirl of white noise. Fastening on to the muffled beat, I realize that it's my own pulse, and around this single clue the order of things resolves. I'm lying on my side; I'm thinking about a JG Ballard story called "Track 12," in which a man dies to the susurrations of his own grossly amplified kiss, and from this stubborn thought I grope my way back: to the pub, to the screens, to Ballard. To Gennison. I'm lying on the floor of his study.

You might think my next question would be "How did I

get here?" But I remember perfectly well how I got here. The barkeep rang last call and Gennison suggested a nightcap at his place. "Just around the corner, right on the square," he said. "Show you my Ballard firsts while we're at it," he added with a self-deprecating grimace.

I take in a deep, shuddering breath and open my eyes. I make out the black and white pattern of the rug. About a yard away this pattern vanishes beneath a coagulating pool of black-red blood, which I stare at for a short eternity, until I'm certain its tide is not advancing. I dare not wonder whether the blood is mine, not yet. A few sheets of paper are stuck to the surface of the pool. It smells of salt and cheese.

I try to remember when I had the first intimation that Gennison was mad. But my thoughts won't stick, and the question persists: how on earth did we get on to Ballard? Surely none of this would have happened if we hadn't.

IF YOU LOVE TO READ, favourite books and authors are at the back of every conversation, waiting for their cue, the slightest pretext to join the fray. Many of my youthful friendships, and courtships too, only gained altitude when one of us artlessly guided the chatter to a writer or title we loved. Much later, in the general shakedown that is middle age, one looks at the friendships and relationships thus forged and questions, at last, the accuracy of literary taste as a predictor of like-mindedness.

Perhaps the question is moot. Gennison was a fanatic. He no

doubt had a thousand different strategies for slipping Ballard in. Turning conversations to Ballard was the man's specialty, perhaps his *raison d'etre*. He could probably do it in such a way that left you thinking you were the one who'd done it.

Still, memory insists on churning over the evening for a clue. One minute I was nursing my drink, the next I was smiling faintly as my neighbour at the bar merrily jabbered on about JG Ballard.

Gennison was roughly my age, 45, a balding chap with watery eyes, round cheeks and a bushy moustache. He wore a tan trench coat over a dark brown suit that was fraying at the cuffs and bronze at the knee, like a statue rubbed for good luck by generations of passers-by. I would have guessed he was a salesman, an area rep for a pharmaceuticals firm perhaps. It turned out his game was civil engineering.

I laughed when he told me this. "You've got me there."

His eyes showed confusion. But he was eager to avoid giving any hint of offense and he quickly shaped his lips into a weak smile. "Er, not sure I follow," he apologized.

"Your profession. It's the profession of an archetypal Ballard character," I said, faintly impatient. "I'd have to be a psychiatrist to trump you."

"Yes, now that you mention it there are rather a lot of them in his stories, aren't there?" He forced a laugh, and then fell silent. "So good to meet a fellow enthusiast," he sighed into the conversational pause.

I make no apologies for being proprietorial, as I'm of that very small cadre of readers who've actually suffered for Ballard. As a spotty teen back in the seventies heyday of British fandom I bore the brunt of some cheap shots from the spaceships and robots crowd, who ran Jim down at every chance. The mainstream was a lost cause then, though of course no sooner had the literary world begrudged James Graham a measure of respect than the bifurcated penis set came along to claim him as one of their own.

Gennison claimed to have fought the good fight too, but as our conversation ran on I began to suspect he was a latecomer. For one who, moments before, had been crowing on about surgical precision in prose, he showed a damnable impreci-sion about short story titles: it was "the one about the dying astronaut" or "that one with the family members who kill each other when they finally meet in person." I'm not petty about these things in small doses but after the fourth or fifth time my irritation surfaced.

"Another classic is the one about the motorway," I said.

"But... but that could be any of them. Oh, I see!" He laughed at what he took to be a joke, as fearful of taking offense as he was of giving it.

I LIE ON THE FLOOR in Gennison's study, listening intently to the silence suppurate through his house. Somewhere a spring-driven mantle clock whirrs like frantic beetle trapped in glass and rings out the hour. Midnight. Only midnight. Whatever madness erupted forth was cataclysmic, immediate, and, to gauge from the silence in the house, conclusive. Where is Gennison?

An hour ago I was holding the door of the pub open for him. Fifty-five minutes ago we were strolling through the youthful mayhem of Friday night, two middle aged men tacking gently, mildly under the influence of drink. Occasionally our separate weaving courses converged and we bumped shoulders. Another five minutes and we had entered Gennison's narrow house on the square, where he deposited me in a spotless but rather desolate front room while he trotted off for a bottle.

At the far end of the room a set of French doors opened into a second room, pitch black. In the darkness, at floor level, the green LEDs of a cable modem briefly flickered at a burst of network activity—a carrier's touch, or the port scan of a hacker. In the assumption that this must be Gennison's study, I stepped through the doorway and groped for a lamp standing just inside.

I found myself in a sublime iteration of that most pallid of fantasy rooms, the learned man's library. "Fantastic," I said aloud as I took in the details of this cozy chamber. An antique globe the size of a medicine ball on a gleaming oak pedestal. A rack of pipes on one wall, purely ornamental in that there was no hint of tobacco in the air. The walls were Manly Blue and seemed to recede in embarrassment at the burden of etchings and oils they bore. I drifted to the desk. Queued up on the back edge was a set of miniature die-cast satellites that must have dated from the sixties. Not simply nostalgic for the collective past, Gennison evidently longed for his own childhood too, and for the future as it would have seemed to a boy admiring his rockets forty years ago.

The walls on either side of the desk were lined with books. I moved towards the shelves with a sense of foreboding.

The library was devoted entirely to Ballard, and contained multiple editions, in many languages, of almost every title the man had published. Even the exceedingly rare first Gollancz printing of *The Drowned World*. There were also Advanced Reading Copies, Uncorrected Galleys, and the like. On the lower shelves were magazines in which Ballard's stories had first appeared, stretching back to sci-fi pulps from the sixties and seventies.

I noticed several framed pieces of correspondence nearby and stepped over for a closer look. They were bits of Ballard ephemera—a note from the man to his agent promising an unnamed ms. in two weeks time, a letter from his editor at Cape apologizing for a publication delay. There was also a photo of Ballard with John Malkovich on the set of *Empire of the Sun*.

I took a step back, and looked at the library afresh. Who but the author himself would reasonably be expected to possess such an exhaustive collection, yet one peppered with banalities of no intrinsic interest? I pictured Gennison seated at his desk, fingering his Sputnik, adrift in a dissociative fugue. He wasn't just trying to collect Ballard: he was trying to be him.

I heard footsteps, and stiffened, as though I'd been caught rifling a porn stash.

"Ah!" said Gennison behind me as he entered the study. "You've found the Ballardiana."

"Yes," I said. I was reluctant to turn around, lest I find that he had changed into Ballard kit and drag.

"Tidy little St. Emilion," said Gennison as he uncorked a bottle with some sort of hydraulic device that went off with a muffled retort. "Shame about what's happening in Bordeaux. EU paying the old firms to plough the vineyards under." We were seated in the corner in a pair of velvet wingchairs. Gennison's hand shook as he leaned over to pour wine. He snuck a nervous glance at me, but his eyes quickly darted away when they met my own cool appraisal.

I suppose I felt a twinge of pity: he must have believed that he'd found in me a sympathetic audience for his tawdry secret life. But he'd miscalculated, and he seemed to know it. His fumbling attempt to change the topic of conversation, to prove that he could talk about something other than Ballard, was an obvious ploy to counter the evidence of monomania surrounding us.

"Ballard still lives in a bungalow near Shepperton," I said. I sipped the wine. He was right; it wasn't shabby. "I doubt his study looks anything like this." The wave of my hand was unmistakably contemptuous, but when Gennison responded, it was by smiling. He had absorbed the contempt and appeared chagrined, but there was confusion in his eyes.

"Well, yes, no doubt he'd find a room like this rather trite. Faded dreams of Oxbridge I suppose."

Suddenly it was all pouring out, as though what he really wanted when he invited me back from the pub was not a fellow enthusiast, but a confessor. "A collection does rather sneak up on you. I didn't set out to collect Ballard, just found myself acquiring Modern Firsts. Having dropped a few more quid than I should have I thought it best to learn the ropes before I blew it all—a small inheritance from my father—and what they tell you, 'they' being, as 'they' always are, those who might be expected to know such things, at any rate what they tell you is to choose a niche that's of inherent interest to you. Because chances are you're going to be repeatedly and royally buggered by the very blokes giving you the self-same advice, and that being the case, you might as well own some books that you'd bloody well like to *read*, because you sure as hell won't be selling them for profit. Not in your lifetime nor that of your heirs." He flashed a quick smile, a weak and rather pitiful invitation for me to smile along. "Anyway, so I thought Golden Age Sci-Fi would do it, but it's all priced out, then took a look at the English New Wave, more affordable but far too much to keep track of for a duffer such as me. So I settled for Ballard.

Prolific enough that one will never have it all, which would quite defeat the purpose wouldn't it? Enough mainstream recognition—Hollywood and all that—that he's not likely to sink into utter jumble sale obscurity. Still producing, with the resulting appeal of new Firsts at less-than-list. And with the happy added benefit that I actually like the stuff."

He'd been counting off the reasons to collect Ballard on his fingers. Now he waved his hand at the groaning shelves with a gesture of such feigned indifference that I could no longer hold in my loathing at his evasions and hypocrisies.

"How much can you *like* a two line note to his editor?"

He was flummoxed and tried to outsource responsibility with another appeal to the natural 'momentum' of a collection, but he veered off when he saw that I was having none of it.

"You're making too much of it," he pleaded. "Those were just sitting in the case at the counter in a shop. In Tunsbridge Wells if I recall. I wasn't even buying Ballard! Some nonsense about wizards for my youngest."

That bit, I admit, took me aback. "You have children?" I glanced around as though the wretches might emerge from beneath the furniture. "A wife?"

"Three of the former. An ex of the latter." He bowed his head and drew in his lips, catching the lower fringes of his moustache too. I remembered, for no reason, that when I was a child I liked to hold my toothbrush under the running tap and then suck the water from its bristles. For some reason the water tasted better that way. What would Gennison's whiskers taste like? Stale ale, tangy sweat, and salt and grease and vinegar from the chips he'd been eating in the pub.

Now he looked up at me again. "I suppose it's why I got started in the entire collecting business. The Bordeaux." He waved at the shelves again, this time the motion communicating an utter exhaustion. "The Ballards. Lot of new holes to fill in the evening." His gaze moved past me to the books. At last the desperate, appeasing expression drained away and he sagged in desolation and confusion.

I AM LYING ON THE FLOOR in a man named Gennison's study. I don't take my eyes off the clotting pool of blood a foot from my face, lest it creep towards me and engulf me. I haven't moved.

Gradually the last and most elusive of the senses returns to me: proprioception, that inner awareness one has of one's own body. I close my eyes, the better to concentrate, and I'm rewarded with a profound awareness of my own mind. The warmth spreading through me is mind itself flowing into my torso and limbs to reclaim its full allotment of clay.

I feel no pain. I wiggle my toes, and smile. "Careful," I chide myself, wary that this sense of well-being may be mere propaganda spread by natural opiates in response to grievous harm. And then I do receive an unnerving message. I seem to be in a semi-foetal position, with my hands tucked down near my groin. One of them is wrapped around a something smooth and tubular, something that feels warm and comfortable in my palm. I raise my left hand.

My cheek chafes against the rug as I cry out in alarm: my hand is covered in blood.

I JUMP TO MY FEET, keeping my right hand pressed against my groin, in case it should prove that I'm holding my own butchered member in place. I gape down in horror at myself. From the tunnel of my hand's grip emerges a mangled vortex of bloody matter. A few hairs stick to this mess.

Then a gleam of light reflects from the bloody stump in my grip. I raise my hand and I discover that I'm grasping the neck of a wine bottle. I relax my hold on it and study it in my outstretched palm.

The bottle has shattered; around the base of the green shaft, like a corolla of angry petals, are jagged shards of glass from the shoulders of the bottle. These shards are painted with blood, yet the effect, now that my surge of panic has passed, is one I find almost beautiful, and I am obliquely reminded of Count Axel snapping crystalline flowers by their glass stems in his doomed compound.

I hear Gennison's voice in memory.

"We're all like the old fellow in that garden, when you get right down to it. You know, the one where every time he picks a magic flower time stutters backwards and the barbarous army recedes."

Suddenly light-headed, I take a step to catch my balance, and there is Gennison, flat on his back, surrounded by pages torn from a book, some of which are stuffed into his mouth.

"*The Garden of Time*, you idiot, The Garden of bloody Time!"

The voice, recalled, is mine, and the sucking sound, the terrible sucking sound I hear all around me, is the present, rushing back in.

ABOUT THE AUTHOR

DAVID HULL WAS BORN in Regina and grew up in Owen Sound, Ontario. His work has appeared in The Walrus, The National Post, Canadian Literature, ON SPEC, and other journals, including Prairie Fire as winner of its long fiction competition. A father of one, he lives in Toronto.

DUMAGRAD BOOKS PRESENTS

THE METAPHYSICAL DICTIONARY
Svetlana Lilova
late 2015

AT GERBER'S GRAVE
A novel
David Hull
early 2016

Buy Dumagrad books:
dumagrad.com

Or follow us:
twitter.com/dumagrad
facebook.com/dumagrad

Share your thoughts at Goodreads:
http://bit.ly/1GAhKKj